The Visitors Who Came to Stay

Annalena McAfee
and
Anthony Browne

Hamish Hamilton · London

Katy and her Dad lived alone together in a house by the sea. It was a big house so Katy had a playroom, where her toys slept, as well as her own bedroom. Even Earl, their cat, had a room to himself. Well, it was more of a large cupboard really, but Earl was very proud of it.

Every evening they would watch TV together and then Dad and Katy took turns to read to each other before bed. Dad's favourite story was *Just William,* because that was his name. Katy's favourite was *What Katy Did Next.*

Each morning Dad got Katy off to school and made her
packed lunch: cheese sandwiches and an apple on
Mondays and Fridays; ham sandwiches and an orange on
Tuesdays and Thursdays, and peanut butter sandwiches and
a banana on Wednesdays. He made breakfast for Katy and
Katy put out breakfast for Earl: a runny boiled egg for Katy
and tinned rabbit with added vitamins for Earl.

Weekends with Dad were the most fun. Katy made Dad's breakfast: a bowl of cereal and a cup of coffee. Dad took his turn to feed Earl. After breakfast they would walk through the park and Katy would sit on the roundabout. Dad pushed her so hard that she felt giddy when she got off and pretended to be drunk all the way to the beach. Then they would sit quietly.

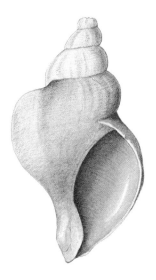

Sometimes Katy went to see her Mum, who lived in another town. She would pack her overnight bag with a nightie, a toothbrush, a change of clothes and Ted. Then on Fridays, after school, she and Dad would catch a train which took them to the big, bustling station in Mum's town. Outside Mum's flat, Katy would kiss Dad goodbye then stand on tiptoes and press the chiming doorbell. On Sundays, after tea, Dad would collect Katy and bring her home.

But apart from those occasional weekends with Mum, Katy spent most of her time with Dad — and she liked it that way.

Then one day things changed. Dad brought home a new friend. Katy and her Dad weren't alone anymore.

"This is Mary," he said. Mary had the widest smile Katy had ever seen. "And this is Sean."

"Like a sweet?" asked Sean. Katy, who never usually ate sweets between meals because Dad said it spoiled her appetite, was too polite to refuse.

"Yeeuch!" It was hot. She spat it into her hand. It looked like a sweet but tasted just like a vindaloo curry that Dad had let her try once. Sean was grinning now, a grin nearly as wide as Mary's.

"It's a joke sweet," he explained.

"Very funny, I *don't* think," said Katy.

Soon Sean and Mary became regular visitors and Katy had to put up with lots of Sean's jokes. He left soap that turned your face black in the bathroom, brought rubber snakes and spiders and put sugar lumps that turned into thick blobs of foam in Dad's tea.

"Very funny, I *don't* think," said Katy.

Earl was not particularly impressed by the visitors either, especially not by Scruff, Sean and Mary's mongrel. Only Dad seemed to be pleased every time Sean and Mary came to visit.

Weekends changed. The visitors would join in Dad's walk with Katy and they would go to the funfair. They ate candyfloss and had to shout to make themselves heard over the blaring pop music and the squeals and shrieks coming from the Waltzer and the Ghost Train.

One weekend Sean and Mary came to stay. Mary carried an old straw picnic hamper crammed full of clothes, and Sean had a battered duffle bag. Sean was to sleep in the spare bed, in Katy's playroom. Scruff made herself at home in Earl's room. Suddenly Katy and Dad's big house seemed small.

Mary seemed to have more clothes than a dress shop: flower print dresses, striped skirts, spotted blouses, multi-coloured jumpers, snakeskin boots, silver slippers, ballet shoes, Smartie coloured berets and a big straw hat with pink felt flowers. They filled Dad's wardrobe. As for Sean, he pulled so many tricks out of his bag you would have thought he was a conjuror. There was sneezing powder, itching powder, a rubber fried egg and a monster's hand with warts.

"Very funny, I *don't* think," said Katy.

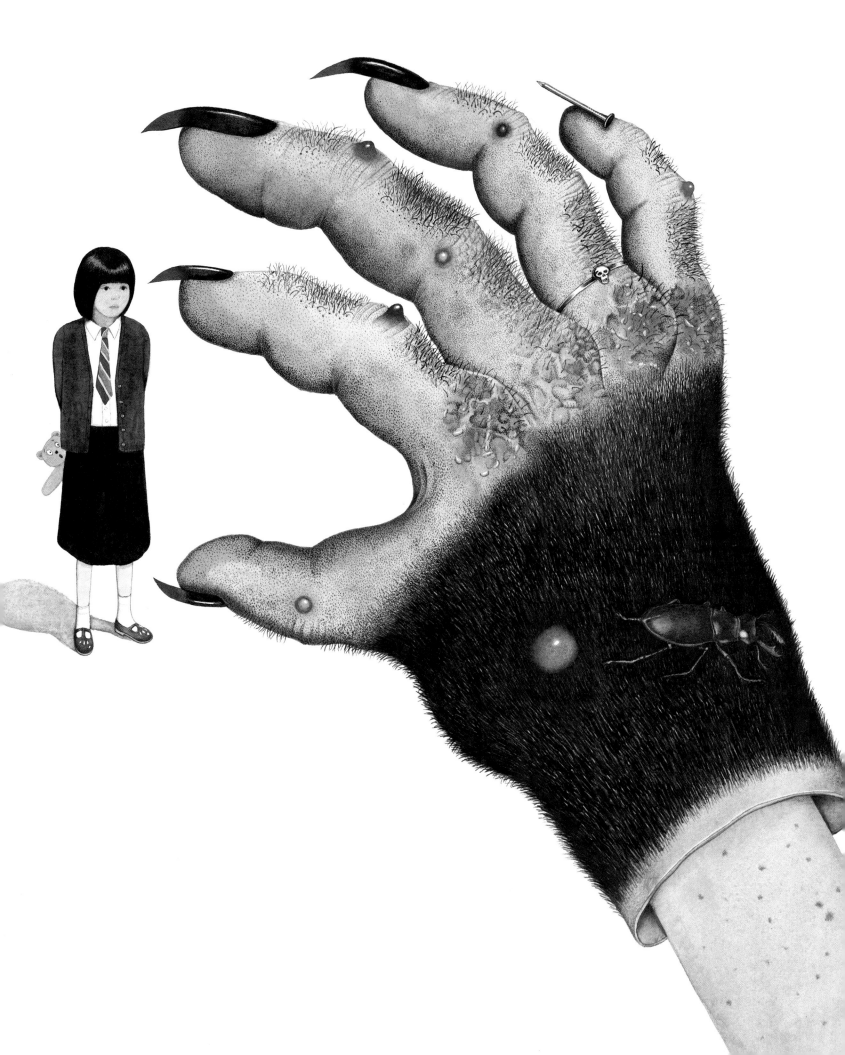

Sean's jokes and Mary's clothes seemed to fill the house. Sometimes Katy felt that she was the visitor, not them. Everything had changed.

Mary helped to make Katy's packed lunch every morning and she always got it wrong. She made peanut butter sandwiches on Mondays instead of Wednesdays and gave her a pear and a chocolate biscuit instead of a banana. Mary helped Dad make breakfast and she seemed to use every pot, pan and plate. There was always a huge pile of dirty dishes in the sink and on the draining board. She made fried eggs with black frills instead of proper boiled eggs.

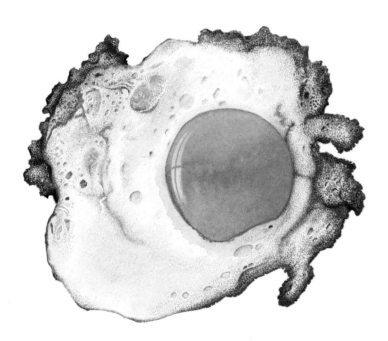

Weekends weren't like weekends anymore. Mary and Sean couldn't just take a simple walk to the beach like Katy and Dad. They seemed to bring half the house with them. There would be enough food to feed nearly everyone on the beach: bottles of lemonade, wine, a flask of coffee, four towels, a hat, books, suntan oil, a bucket and spade, a tablecloth and at least one joke for Sean. On the way they'd stop off at the amusement arcade and feed pennies into the fruit machines. Then Mary would insist that they all have ice creams. On the beach Mary wouldn't sit still but would chat and laugh with Dad.

"Dad, do you see what I see?" asked Katy. But Dad didn't hear.

Often, Katy found it a relief to get home and snatch some peace upstairs with her toys. But even then Sean would come in and want to play with her.

"What on earth is that?" Katy asked as he produced a small rubber cushion from his bag.

"It's a Whoopee Cushion," Sean explained. "You blow it up and leave it on a chair. When someone sits on it, it makes the rudest noise you've ever heard." He demonstrated by forcing air out of the cushion with his hands. Katy blushed. He was right — it was the rudest sound imaginable.

Katy went to tell Dad but he was in a hurry to go out with Mary. Mrs Murray had come round to look after Sean and Katy. She was an old babysitter who always put children to bed early so she could watch television.

"Why can't I come too?" Katy asked Dad.

"It's only for grownups," he said with his arm round Mary. Dad just didn't seem to be the same Dad any more.

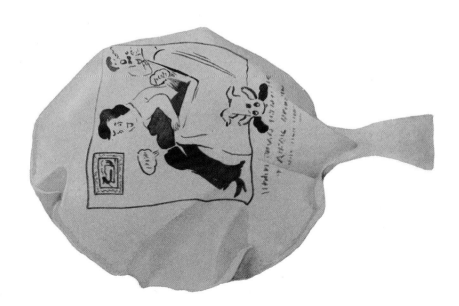

Katy was fed up. She didn't like sharing her house, her garden, her toys, her walks and her meals. She didn't like sharing her Dad, and one day she told him so.

The next morning when Katy went downstairs for breakfast she sensed that something strange had happened. The house seemed quiet and empty. Sean and Mary were standing in the hall with their bags packed. They were leaving. They kissed Katy and Dad goodbye and shut the front door behind them. Katy sighed with relief and leaned heavily against the front door.

"Phew!" she said, looking at Dad, "it's nice to have the house to ourselves again."

It was good to have Dad get her off to school alone each day and to read together and play together, just the two of them. Katy was glad they had their old weekends back to themselves. Soon it was just like old times — well almost. Earl seemed delighted to have his room back too. Only Dad seemed a little quieter and more thoughtful than usual.

Gradually Katy and Dad slipped back into their familiar routine. But one night, Katy got an odd feeling that something was not quite right. She was playing with her toys in the playroom when she suddenly felt something was missing. She checked all her toys, but they were all there. Then she looked in every room to see if she could find a clue to what was missing. Still no luck. As she watched television that night with Dad she couldn't stop thinking about it. What on earth was it that she'd lost?

It wasn't until the next day, when Dad suggested "How about paying Sean and Mary a visit?" that Katy realised what she'd been missing. Now she thought about it, life with the visitors hadn't been so bad. She missed Sean's jokes, especially the Whoopee Cushion that he'd left for Mrs Murray to sit on one night when she was babysitting. Katy missed Mary's smile, and her clothes had been particularly useful for dressing up. There was, after all, a limit to the amount of dressing up you could do with Dad's old shirts and a few ties. Katy realised that she didn't mind sharing Dad, or her house, or her toys, or her walks, if she could share Sean and Mary too.

"Yes," said Katy, "let's visit Sean and Mary!" But as they walked up the garden path to Sean and Mary's house, Katy made sure she had a surprise in store for Sean — she was going to take his picture with a very special camera, bought that morning from a joke shop. "Smile please," she would say before pressing the button. It would squirt a jet of water right between Sean's eyes. She couldn't wait to see his face.

First Published in Great Britain 1984 by
Hamish Hamilton Children's Books
27 Wrights Lane, London W8 5TZ

Paperback edition first published 1987
Text copyright © Annalena McAfee 1984
Illustrations copyright © Anthony Browne 1984
All Rights Reserved

British Library Cataloguing in Publication Data
McAfee, Annalena
The Visitors who came to stay
I. Title II. Anthony Browne
823'.914[J]   PZ7
Hardback ISBN 0-241-11224-9
Paperback ISBN 0-241-12018-7

Printed in Hong Kong by
South China Printing Co